The
Ballad of
Johnny
Sosa

The Ballad of Johnny Sosa

A NOVEL BY

Mario Delgado Aparaín

Translated from the Spanish by Elizabeth Hampsten

THE OVERLOOK PRESS
Woodstock & New York

First published in the United States in 2002 by
The Overlook Press, Peter Mayer Publishers, Inc.
Woodstock & New York

WOODSTOCK:
One Overlook Drive
Woodstock, NY 12498
www.overlookpress.com
[for individual orders, bulk and special sales, contact our Woodstock office]

NEW YORK:
141 Wooster Street
New York, NY 10012

∞ The paper used in this book meets the requirements for paper
permanence as described in the ANSI Z39.48-1992 standard.

Library of Congress Cataloging-in-Publication Data

Aparaín, Mario Delgado.
[Balada de Johnny Sosa. English]
The ballad of Johnny Sosa : a novel / by Mario Delgado Aparaín;
translated from the Spanish by Elizabeth Hampsten.
p. cm.
I. Hampsten, Elizabeth.   II. title
PQ8520.14.E45 B313 2002   863'.64—dc21   2002020604

Book design and type formatting by Bernard Schleifer
Printed in the United States of America
ISBN 1-58567-224-6
10 9 8 7 6 5 4 3 2 1

"Ai nid tubí fri

uit iú ander de trí.

Bat aiam an only man

an only blak man,

an . . . ou, beiby"

From "Melancholy on Your Knees"

The Ballad of Johnny Sosa

*I*T WOULD HAVE BEEN ON ONE OF THE LAST NORMAL days when Johnny Sosa, the Black, was still able to get excited looking through the chink in the adobe wall to wait, anxious as a child, for *The Fertile Hour in the Early Dawn*.

Those were the times when, torn between sleep and the tiny crack, he would divine more than actually see the blue silhouettes of the last houses of Mosquitos. Lined up along the road north to nowhere, and shaken by the wild swaying of the eucalyptus trees, these dwellings might well have been wrapped in invisibility, so formless were they that Johnny had to force his eye in the hole and ask himself in the gravelly voice of the just-awakened, whether the scene swinging out and snapping back before him was composed of houses, shadows, or trucks.

Sometimes the darkness was so thick that, try as he might, he could see nothing more through the hole than familiar dogs outlined by their barking, which, for him, was just as well. When things were like that and the weather truly bad, he'd settle into the tiny chair, his hands around the fresh hot *mate*, kettle near his toes, and pass the time with one eye dreamily closed and the other probing mysteries through the hole, as to whether the shadows be houses or trucks, until at last it came time to turn on the two-battery Spika radio and shake himself out of his daydreams.

Religiously from that moment on, from seven to eight o'clock, with nothing and no one to bother him, while blonde Dina slept on the other side of the sackcloth curtain talking in her sleep, Johnny gave himself over to listening to the biography of Lou Brakley and guessing how long it might take for his life to unfold into a similar story.

Spurred by incidents in the latest episodes, Johnny had been thinking that in certain respects the two childhoods did indeed resemble each other. It hardly mattered that he had not, at age eight, won a guitar in a contest on the theme of summer, as had the great one from Austin in the face of the cruel indifference of his father, a cross-eyed man devoted to drink and to the Bible, who, according to the narrator, would fritter away the working day and then get soundly beaten up in bars, while his wife, that is to say the mother of Lou, waited for him in vain, ironing furiously, long into the night.

Johnny supposed such lives took shape only in a country like Lou Brakley's. He suspected that here, hard as he might have tried for it when he was ten or twelve years old, he would never have been given the chance to perform in recording festivals or on one of the Gold Coast beaches, such as The Titans or Shangri-La, distant resorts inhabited by the sons of Cary Grant, about which he had heard when coast-to-coast festivals began to be popular, and with them also the names of the winners.

Nor was it likely that a music scout would land in Mosquitos, inquiring in the Euskalduna bar, his mouth full of *milanesa*, for the whereabouts of one Johnny Sosa, whose reputation as an angel with a golden throat had reached the ears of the scout. If only it were, it would be easy for Johnny to fit himself into the legend that ran through the city of Austin, according to the narrator Melías Churi, about how Lou Brakley was discovered by a man who had spent two years looking for someone with a Black man's dreams, a Black's sentiments, the voice of a Black, but who, of necessity, had to be white.

"That will never happen in Mosquitos," he'd laugh and scold himself, alone in his kitchen. Simply because he was black. And from then on, nothing to do with Lou Brakley. And even less probable was the chance of a recording of his own. He supposed it would be a couple of centuries at least before it occurred to anyone in the little town to set up one of those do-it-yourself studios, the spot where apparently the scout had come upon the lucky Austin boy rehearsing a wicked version of a blues tune by Arthur "Big Boy" Crudup, called "That's All Right (Mama)."

According to what the announcer of *The Fertile Hour in the Early Dawn* had said, that was exactly what the veteran star-catcher had been looking for. And just like that, while Johnny listened with his mind aswim in a parallel life, the announcer had taken a great leap into the empty space of time, yanked the boy out of his pathetic anonymity, and placed him in the time in which Lou Brakley became, before the eyes of the world, nothing less than Lou Brakley.

"Nevertheless, 1956 had to have been a hard year for the singer," Melías Churi had declared in the previous episode. "But that stage in the life of the author and interpreter of "The One-Star Motel" we shall hear tomorrow, dear listeners, God willing, at seven o'clock on Radio Mosquitos."

At five minutes to seven the road was still dark under its plaster of cold mud, and trees were beginning to take on the crazed profiles of early dawn, thanks to a wind savage enough to make dogs take off howling in all directions.

Johnny strained to make out an actual shape. For all he forced his eyes, it made him nervous not to be able to tell at exactly what point they stopped being shadows or trucks and became what they truly were. A dark line, both movable and static, invariably reduced him to a dull stupor abated only by the hot *mate* and was gone altogether as soon as he turned on the little radio and closed up the crack in the wall.

Then he cast a last glance at the old figure of Cronos, standing like a fat sawmill foreman on the label of the *mate* can. He set the *mate* gourd carefully over the open mouth of the kettle and then, with a few brief sips as preludes to the morning's pleasure, he turned on the small red Spika.

His face quickly lost that mild expression anticipating a pleasant start to the morning. Music burst into the quiet kitchen, cockroaches scuttled under shelf linings, and Johnny blinked. He thought he had turned the dial to the wrong station or that Dina had changed the time on the big clock, or maybe Melías Churi had overslept and in the crisis this inexplicable music was substituting for his *Fertile Hour in the Early Dawn*.

It also might be otherwise, that the musical barrage had to do with an unforeseen episode in the life of the great one from Austin, such as occurred on the sad Christmas when Lou Brakley was beaten to a pulp by his father and the announcer began the program one morning in March with the sound of sleigh bells in a beautiful string arrangement of "Jingle Bells" performed by native Hawaiians.

While the band grew ever louder with heroic intrusions by the trombones, Johnny took a deep breath and returned to casting his eye through the hole. He waited patiently, supposing with growing certainty that it all might be related to the amazing episode of Lou Brakley's life, when at the end of '57 the singer from Austin joined the Eisenhower boys, and newspapers world-wide showed the outrage committed on his splendid mane as it was mowed by a Green Beret barber to get him ready for whatever war on the planet he might be called to, while outside the barber shop a group of girls wept as if they were witnessing the beheading Lou Brakley in San Quentin.

But actually that story had been announced by Melías Churi for two or three episodes farther ahead, and there had not been the slightest indication of what would be happening in the life of the splendid boy on this particular day, when the military march was turning into a cacophony that would never stop.

So Johnny came to accept as fact that the music had no relation to the life of Lou Brakley, but rather reminded him of the afternoon *The Bridge on the River Kwai* was shown in the Daguerre movie house, and Capozoli had hung a chain of loudspeakers the length of the block so that townspeople would hear the movie's military march and come at a quick-step to the five o'clock showing.

But the theater owner had been so dazzled by the famed intransigence of the English prisoner that he sat on a stool on the sidewalk against the first loudspeaker and devoted himself to drinking warm beer and listening to the endless march, arms across his chest, as if waiting, with dignity worthy of Alec Guinness, for the

Japanese to come storming down Ellauri street, bayonets between their teeth. That night, after the last show was over and Capozoli still sat surrounded by beer bottles, the police had to tell him to turn off the infernal racket, because from the River Kwai to Mosquitos, no Christian would be able to sleep.

In the meantime, while all this was going through Johnny's head, Dina appeared in the kitchen with her sideways glance and flowered panties and put a stop to the mad quivering of the two-battery radio. In an icy tone she asked whether the Battle of Las Piedras was being re-enacted, or on this freezing morning in June had Capozoli taken over the Mosquitos radio station?

But Johnny neither reacted to her half-nude state, her skin rough with goosebumps from the cold draft seeping through the cracks, nor did he say, "Good morning my blondie," as he always did, nor even appear to listen to whatever she had been saying. He remained absent, concentrating his single eye at the chink in the adobe, only without seeing the confusing shapes that he was used to seeing.

"They are not houses," he said without surprise.

And because Black Johnny was truly looking, and what he was seeing really was occurring, he removed his eye from the crack and opened the other the better to take in Dina's state of undress.

"Go get dressed," he said. "This time they're trucks."

*T*HE ARMY TRUCKS DID NOT ENTER THE LITTLE TOWN. They remained in the same place where the dark clouds of that morning in June had drawn them, lined up under the row of eucalyptus. They stood there, cold as monuments, mysterious, without anyone's getting out of them to modify the scene.

Then at dawn on the second day a clutch of enormous gray tents appeared, as though brought from a sorry Brazilian circus about to give its last performance, and almost concealed the vehicles.

Startled by the early morning bugle call, on the first days residents on the edge of town went out to their patios and scratched their ribs considerably earlier than was their habit. *Mate*s in hand, they crowded against the fences and pointed at the strenuous maneuvers of soldiers climbing the frozen hill over thorns and on their bellies and commented nervously about the furious shooting, astonished to think battles could be arranged to begin at nine in the morning and finish exactly at dinner time. Actually, people were only guessing, exchanging imprecise calculations as they tried to fathom what those men were up to, acting as if they were alone in the middle of a desert heedless to the puzzlement they left in their wake. Nor could the residents come closer than a couple of blocks from the encampment, thanks to the cordon of stern guards in green ponchos and battle gear encircling the field, shouting to each other and oblivious to anything else.

"Each chooses the life that suits him," Dina said one morning, in a practical turn of mind, as she abandoned the wire fence and went back to her kitchen.

While no one was allowed to cross the area nor even felt they were due an explanation, residents of Mosquitos were paying an unfairly high price. More than once, Johnny Sosa had to give up his place between Dina's legs and blow out the candle, because soldiers were adventuring among the shacks, slithering along the walls, to pop a gap-toothed face at the windowpane and frighten the inhabitants.

Then they'd leave, disappearing into the darkness without having knocked on a single door, never saying why they were trampling through gardens with their enormous boots.

"The next one that shows up at the window or sticks his hoof in the flower beds, I'll crack his head open with an ax," Johnny threatened, furious, on one of the first nights a pair of hairy eyebrows steaming from the cold surprised him on the other side of the pane.

"They're sick," said Dina, and went back to sleep.

As Johnny was not made for mystery, nor adhered to things divine, on the following Saturday, when warm vapors could be seen rising from the mud along the road, he asked Dina how serious did she think this was: that from one day to the next, people's ordinary conversations should turn muddled, or Rulo the grocer be more mute than the echoes of his own foot steps and above all, that the life of Lou Brakley should have stopped on the airwaves of Mosquitos.

"The best anyone can do is stay where they are," she answered, going back to looking out the dark window. "As my mother used to say, 'Jesus, enough to eat, and nobody come to the table that isn't already here.'"

Johnny did not know what to say to that. But while he brought order to his wiry mop with the comb made of bone, he promised that night he'd bring fresh news from the Chanteclere, for surely in the early hours of the end of the week Terelú would have something to tell him of the evil story.

Nevertheless, he couldn't decide whether to go or stay, get dressed or wait a little longer in case a sign came that he might go in peace. He stood for a moment looking gloomily at the weak lock on the door and remarked that he was afraid to leave Dina alone at the mercy of marauders.

"Don't worry. They have no way of knowing how bad our doors are," she said, trying to be cheerful, her voice encouraging him to once more show off his black wool windbreaker and the mariner's saint on its fake silver chain around his neck.

Johnny knew enough to appreciate her show of good will. Their fiercest quarrels occurred early on Saturday mornings, when he'd return from the night's work to discover that the devil had poisoned his blonde in her solitary hours into imagining pettings and raptures from the whores who felt that Johnny was singing to them.

"It's a job like any other," he'd say in his defense every Saturday before going out, confident that, in this area, matters always would go better for him than for poor Lou Brakley, an artist terrified that his women would appear on the stage to cause a holy scandal on the issue of property rights to the heart.

"You are a case, my Black man," said Dina as they parted, a feeble reproach contradicted by her hand squeezing his neck. For she had long since amicably accepted what he did and showed she was impressed by his total blackness, his hair standing up like a horse's mane as if it had lain on a stone pillow, while she held the guitar in its embroidered case in one hand and the little green bongo drum in the other.

Then he would ask why she thought he was "a case," and she would say quietly, as if rebuking someone who was not Johnny, "Not a cent to buy a good spading fork for the garden," she'd say, "but there better be enough for the belt with silver-plated medallions. No bottle of Embrujo perfume for the blonde in this shack, but certainly a pair of embossed pointy-toed boots. And no ointment for the singer's gums, although he's forever thinking of his image and only of his image. That is why I say he's a case, this man."

By the last phrases she'd be trembling against the frame of the open door, while Johnny disappeared down the gravel road neither waving nor turning back, because it was close to time for the performance.

Johnny did not learn until far into the night, just before his demented rendition of "Tutti Frutti," that the man with bottled eyes and hair slicked back and glowing with Glostora oil was none other than the announcer of *The Fertile Hour in the Early Dawn.*

If it had not been for the disquieting impression he gave, as someone on the brink of great fear—marching off to a dozen years in prison, or to death—Melías Churi would have passed for any townsman, perhaps a melancholy enthusiast of brothel histories, hunched in a corner table and of no importance to anyone after midnight.

From the door he looked like he was asleep. From the stage he appeared all too much in existence. But if anyone were to take the trouble to sit across from him at the table, he would find a man adrift, helped along by the women of the night and post office clerks in the adjoining seats, but quite capable on his own of plunging headlong into impending catastrophes.

That he would soon be bound for misfortune, the announcer had not the slightest doubt, and he had known perfectly well he was a dead man drinking *café con leche*, from the moment he encased his head in a woman's stocking and erupted in the heart of the Mosquitos radio station along with two armed cohorts

identified only by their *noms de guerre*. At gun-point
they had forced Fuentes, the announcer, to read a
brief proclamation against the brand-new military
government, which the poor innocent carried out to
the letter, never having suspected all those mornings
that he was sharing rolls and *mate* with the silent
masked figure who was placing before his eyes an
incendiary message.

But Melías Churi's confidence in no one's being
able to tell the source of the careful handwriting in
which the proclamation was written had weakened
steadily from the moment the short man in the bristling
mustache began following him from dawn to dusk. The
only investigator of the Mosquitos police force who still
believed in the efficacy of civilian clothing, that character nevertheless had broken the rules of job secrecy, for,
standing like a post at the bar of the Chanteclere, there
was nothing discreet in the way he watched the
announcer, letting him know he had every intention of
screwing up his life down to the ultimate conse-
quences.

With no intention of losing sight of the vacuous face that so got on his nerves, on the dot of twelve Melías Churi relaxed enough to let himself be swept away by the wiles of that Black on the red platform offering himself up as the true way to the soul. From his height on the stage, Johnny bowed slowly, then with his left foot pushed the shiny quince jelly tin forward so the card faced the audience, its clear, even letters reading, "voluntary contributions."

Then, guitar across his chest in the style of a roaming minstrel, he waited for the postal workers to turn around and for María Teresa de Australia to stop showing off her rear and pulling down her bra straps. When he was certain there was no one left who did not know that the magic hour had arrived, Johnny lowered his eyelids, retreated to the back of his cave, and gave the opening yell.

His fist almost closed, he hit the sound box of the Black Diamond and began a slow, grave, intimate pleading, "Dont cruai for a blac jert, beiby, ai seid" ("Don't cry for a black heart, baby, I said"), then lowered the pitch for quick variants in the verse that moved to blues and whistling—a slow half-alive sound, that barely lit up before it dove to the lower belly in a fine, sharp flame, leaving listeners wondering whether what they were hearing was a human creature or a blue shadow.

Melías Churi, wide-eyed, arms stretched across the table, pressed the beer glass between his hands. What he was watching was a horrendous mix of Frankie Avalon, Ray Charles, and the worst of Lou Brakley. But there was no point in pursuing the point. His head was giving out, so he surrendered to a light paralysis anticipating Johnny's humming, a stillness that went beneath the skin, when only the eyes were alive above the almost-dead smile, innocent of teeth in the kidney-shaped lips. In fact it was a good thing, when he neared the approach to "Melancholy on Your Knees," the moment when he held the mysterious aura of the song in suspense, that Johnny changed instruments.

Then he'd set his lethargic winter lizard of a guitar against the stool and warm up the little green bongo drum, all the while howling toward the ceiling of the

Chanteclere a hymn to the wonder of life, which, as the chords descended, turned the women into sorrowing virgins and made them cry.

This was Johnny with other people's sorrows.

"Not like that, you bloody fool! That's not how it goes," Melías Churi shouted above the applause from his table in the corner. The Mosquitos radio announcer raged against the indecipherable idiom of the songs, a language where not even titles contained recognizable words.

When he finished singing, Johnny did not pick up the coins in the quince jelly tin at the edge of the stage right away. He stood with his eyes fixed on the corner table where Melías Churi, bent over his arms, was still shouting, in a progressively weaker voice, that that was not the way to sing. Then Johnny took a deep breath, and all the while rubbing his silver medallion of the mariner saint, stepped off the platform and approached the table, close enough to press Melías Churi's shoulder with his strumming hand.

"What were you saying, friend? What is your problem?" Johnny's tone was aggressive, but the massive hollow mouth devoid of teeth rather weakened the hostility.

Used to speaking at a distance from physical contact, Melías Churi lifted his head in alarm and shook off the hand on his shoulder. His eyes were teary, unfocussed, they swam with anger at having to put up with such wasted effort, although his fury might better have been directed at the world at large than at the Black standing in front of him dressed in a style copied from some from Brooklyn crooner from some movie Capozoli had shown in the Daguerre, since Johnny, if one did not count pilgrimages to the Virgin of Verdún, had never been out of Mosquitos. "What's going on with you?" the black man insisted again.

"You don't do that," said Melías Churi. "Those songs . . ."

"What about those songs?" Johnny asked.

"Nothing," Melías Churi said, infuriated. "That's just it, they're not about anything. That's not English. They aren't anything."

The announcer, chair shoved back abruptly, was

wavering dangerously, but Johnny steadied him, while he brought his mouth to Churi's ear, but before saying anything, kept silent for a beat, in time with the balancing chair.

"Juai nat? Ai laic uoch fil mí forever, ruait" ("Why not? I like you fill me forever, right.") And that, you queer, what's that?" he asked in a frozen whisper out of the corners of his mouth.

The hand that strummed "Melancholy on Your Knees" gripped Churi fast. Added to the hold was a facial expression reminiscent of a solitary gunman from Tierra del Fuego, a down-on-his luck detective, or an alcoholic priest in doubt about the existence of God. "They'd all be there, from two o'clock to seven for who knows how many years of matinees, in that blasted movie house," Churi would say to a prison buddy years later, dredging up bad memories from the eternity of the prison cell.

The announcer brusquely straightened himself up in the chair and picked up his beer. Between swallows he noticed the bushy-whiskered man, who watching from the bar without moving. A lousy detective out of fourth-rate movies, forced by Churi to shift his gaze to an indeterminate point on the shelves, where pale Tomé Cara de Humo was reconstituting bottles of sugar cane with various herbs.

Suddenly the announcer looked Johnny square in the eye and let him have it, "Capozoli, son of seven thousand whores!"

At first Johnny just stood there, his half-opened lips showing surprise, not seeing a connection between the owner of the movie house and the situation at hand. Gradually, he decided there was none, and that this fellow with his head thrown back was just a common drunk, insulting the absent and whoever happened to be present.

"Whore-son yourself," returned Johnny, taking a step forward and now standing above Churi, his fists clenched. "Talking behind someone's back, that's not very manly, I'd say . . . Why don't you go up and say it to Capozoli, eh?"

"Right, Johnny Sosa, that's it: me, son of a whore . . ." Melías Churi insisted with bitter energy. "Sons of whores Capozoli and the Daguerre, son of a whore me and . . . The-fertile-hour-in-the-early-dawn," he added, raising his glass in a toast to the last string of words.

Johnny's eyes turned bright and his fists opened to let fall some invisible sand as he recognized the voice of the Mosquitos radio announcer, the same inflections that put the great Lou Brakley into the case of the small red Spika on the dot of seven o'clock.

"You are Melías Churi?" he asked cautiously.

For an instant the announcer did not answer, nor did he look at him, but hummed a Mormon hymn while looking vaguely, on the other side of the bar, at Tomé Cara de Humo with a dish towel over his arm saying good-bye to Celeste and María Teresa de Australia, two fat ladies dead with sleep on a bad-luck night, who as they left cast a look of plain disdain at the man with the bushy whiskers, now lost in his drink. Still, numb as he was, the fellow gave the impression of being up to a contest between equals, and Melías Churi was acutely aware of him in spite of the fog.

Johnny noticed his tension and cast his eye about

the customers still left in the Chanteclere. But he could find nothing different from other Saturday nights, except for the languor, the deeply tired expression in the eyes of the announcer.

Tomé Cara de Humo came around the bar to their table with two beers on an aluminum tray, and without paying attention to the man from the radio station, asked Johnny if he would be singing again when he finished the bottle.

Johnny assented and sat down at the table, straddling the chair with the back against him.

"You really are Melías Churi?" he asked again.

"Truly and falsely, I have always been so," said the man, pouring drinks for both. His hand shook visibly, like someone about to say something solemn and complicated, but all that came out was, "What you are doing may be very fine, but it is not English."

He was going to add that there was something else important, and in a certain way impeding, the power of his presence, and that was the absence of teeth, depriving Johnny of the requisite crooner's smile. But Churi said nothing. He kept his attention on the sound of a motor running near the Chanteclere, and the rumble of wheels chewing up gravel in the street until the vehicle stopped close to the door.

Johnny watched him impassively. He drank, swallowed once, twice, foam and thoughts. Then he smacked his kidney-shaped lips and asked what the devil had become of Lou Brakley.

The announcer stared at the heavy medallion dangling on the singer's chest and tried earnestly to remember the rest of the story for this Johnny who actually appeared to like it. Melías Churi found it incredible that in this little town there should exist so deprived a soul as to take the trouble to get up every morning merely to listen to him talk about a gringo who had turned his life into a mediocre tragedy. But, observing the man with the bushy whiskers leave the bar and walk with enviable steadiness toward the door, his memory failed. Yet once the agent was gone, Melías Churi gathered his thoughts, stretched his legs under the table, and remembered.

"Lou Brakley died choked on cocaine," he said. "First he lost his voice and then went to live with his mother in a small town in Illinois, smaller than Mosquitos, where he spent his time collecting guns and waiting for his father to kick the bucket . . ."

Johnny rested his chin on the back of the chair and did not take his gaze off the announcer's half-closed eyes. Convinced that any Christian life was grist for a motion picture, he could clearly see the long, straight, dusty street of a town at three in the afternoon. But as the scene was taking longer than it should and beginning to flow confusedly into others full of little streets and nearly redheaded children walking around with cotton candy, Johnny got impatient and urged Churi on.

"And . . . ?" he asked. "What happened next?"

Melías Churi glanced briefly toward the entrance to the brothel, where one of the post office employees was taking tearful leave of his friends, then returned his gaze to the beer glass.

"What happened was the stupid idiot died before his father," Churi said. "One night he went to the bathroom with the book *The Scientific Search for the Face of Jesus.* Before he went in, his mother had warned him not to fall asleep reading. He replied in exactly these words, 'No, mother. I hate to sleep in the bathroom.'"

This time the announcer did not raise his eyes but paused as if he were before the microphone. He went on in a somber tone, "Those were the last words of Lou Brakley. He had become a very fragile person and his life an absolute shambles. Before burying him they found eleven different substances in his blood."

Johnny was shaken. He could see Lou Brakley, thrown back on the toilet and the book lying on the floor near his cold fingers.

"But the old lady didn't call anyone? Couldn't they do *some*thing?" he asked, his tone a heartbroken reproach against the greatest stupidity of all time.

The announcer shook his head, irritated, and cut him off, unblinking. "Brother, this story is trash, of no matter to anyone," he said.

"It matters to me," Johnny shot back.

The landscape of the Chanteclere, drearier by the

hour, suddenly changed, as a couple of soldiers, of the ones who had been stomping through gardens, drew the customers' attention to the door. They were standing on the sidewalk, their rifles resting between their boots, but had not yet made up their minds to go in.

"Why didn't you say all this over the radio?" Johnny asked with certain heat, supposing at the same time that the soldiers would eventually walk into the brothel.

The announcer moved his head forward to the middle of the table, with a hard and angry expression that Johnny would remember all his life as revealing the true Melías Churi, although at times it could look like a mask. Then, up close he whispered, "I didn't say it because there was a *coup d'etat*."

"In Mosquitos?" Johnny asked surprised.

"In the whole world," said the announcer letting out a moan that made his chest push the table forward, who then asked where the devil had Johnny been all this time. Had it never dawned on him to find out why, between night and morning, tree trunks on Fabini Avenue were painted white? Or why so many inhabitants had been seen leaving with suitcases at dawn? Or why boards had been nailed over the doors of the radio station?

Then he returned to his original position, leaned back on the chair, and drained his beer at the precise instant when the man with the bushy whiskers came back as if he had forgotten something. Numbed by the night cold, wiping his nose on a handkerchief folded in quarters, he walked directly to the bar, and without the least sign of a hangover said something to Tomé Cara de Humo.

The announcer leaned over the table again in a pendulum swing to bring the encounter to a close. "Now leave me alone because this isn't for you . . ." His voice was low and firm.

Unsure of how to keep from looking like a failure, Johnny made himself get up and look around to see whether there were enough people to justify a few more songs at this small hour of the morning.

"So Lou Brakley just died," he said in mild surprise, as he walked to the wooden platform with a fateful feeling, thinking that the Black Diamond was stretching out its loyal arm to him as it never had before.

But pale Tomé Cara de Humo cut across his path to say it would be a good idea to stop the show and urge the rest of the late-nighters home.

Johnny said no, adding that a great urge had come over him to give the audience a few more songs, and that was what he was going to do. So he plugged in the guitar's amplifier cable, and with the leather-tooled toe of his boot he shoved to the edge of the stage the quince jelly tin intended for donations.

He stood for a moment looking around the room and inhaling vague intimations of perfume, distant odors of men and tobacco, but it all struck him as infinitely chillier than other Saturday nights.

Just as he was saying that "to close out the night, ladies and gentlemen, I am going to leave you with a familiar composition," the soldiers, who until then had remained on the sidewalk talking among each other, walked with firm steps into the room, flanking an officer in shirt sleeves rolled to the elbows.

They went straight to the corner where the announcer was straining to hear the singer's words, and scarcely a step away, the officer asked sharp and clear if his name were Melías Churi, and added that, if it were, he was to place his hands together on top of the table.

From the vantage point of the stage, without losing sight of what was happening, Johnny struck the boards with his Texan boot heel, counted "uán, chú, trí . . . ," peered through the cigarette smoke, and launched into a furious version of "Tutti Frutti" that shook the squalid walls of the Chanteclere.

The women still remaining at tables got to their feet and began clapping wildly, shouting "Great, little man, great!" while at their backs the Mosquitos radio station announcer was being led away.

Up in front on the stage, Johnny's knees trembled happily, all of him vibrating under the tension of his closed eyes. Sometimes he'd open them a little, but appear not to like what he saw and shut them even tighter, as if like a crazed blind man he wished when he opened them for the last time, at the instant of the final chords, he would not be there but far away from bar and brothel, at the chink in the adobe, waiting to turn on the little red Spika at the dot of seven and tune into the dream all over again.

*O*RDERS FOR THE definitive imposition of authority came just six months after the military detachment first appeared on the outskirts of town, when a group of soldiers in work clothes finished moving Colonel Werner Valerio's household to the center of Mosquitos.

Tired of camp life, this commanding officer decided it was time to abandon those patched gray tents; he sent for his wife and son at Paso de los Toros and went to live in a proper house two or three blocks from the plaza.

Colonel Valeiro's splendid residence, red tile roof and saint's shrine embedded in the wall under the porch roof, had abruptly ceased to belong to an elderly dentist with twisted ideas, who at the end of a few weeks in an unknown jail, yielded up the use of his bones as a final act of atonement for a string of incontrovertible crimes.

The dentist's wife, faced with the daily solitude of the waiting room, as is the way of wives with little sense of their own worth, sold at giveaway prices everything from the dentist's chair to the old clay dwarfs her husband had put in the garden to distract children from the tortures awaiting them.

After the sale, with the look of someone about to embark on a long journey, and without saying good-bye to anyone, the poor woman boarded the afternoon bus and quit Mosquitos, leaving in front of the door of the abandoned house a cross of salt, the sort often placed after a storm to keep out vermin.

But the next day the house was full of people. A first corporal scattered the salt with a single kick, and Colonel Valerio was able to move his family in just two days.

Meanwhile, as though discipline had gone amok, soldiers sprayed the canvas tents with fuel from the trucks and set them afire, yelling and raising a great uproar.

Before the black smoke and the nauseating smell of burning canvas could dissipate, soldiers were constructing wooden barracks, which would be expanded over the years as new permits were obtained. Once varnished, they were enclosed by a gentle wall of *transparentes* (shade trees).

From then on, if they looked hard, the nearest neighbors could distinguish, next to the guard boxes, the dentist's imperturbable dwarfs.

Officers also elected to come to Mosquitos and follow the Colonel's example. From his first days of residence in the center of town, he had made a habit of sitting on his porch in the late afternoon to sip *mate* in a gigantic gourd wrapped in bull's testicle and watch the doings of his officers. Slowly but surely they were buying up houses, to which they brought their wives in cotton print dresses, and then went to work on the town's morale, filling flower beds in the plaza with purple pansies.

Irritable from being cooped up so long in the tents, the soldiers strode off through the town to stretch their legs and within a week were asking for identification from anyone who dared glance sidewise at their helmets and taking the suspicious-looking to the barracks. Once there, it was not unlikely for an unfortunate to be sat in a chair facing the wall and made to listen to the deafening sound of "Martita's Little Spider" ("*La arañita de Martita*"), a Colombian tune that, by order of a twenty-year-old second lieutenant, was to assault the ears for an uninterrupted six hours, before talk was begun with the suspect. Others arrested were hung from the ceiling while repeatedly asked so many questions they'd condemn themselves by false testimony because of the ease with which their replies were misconstrued.

So that was how in Mosquitos, up to then sweetened by years of harmonious poverty and soft gaslight at night, its inhabitants now for the first time crossing the sidewalk in case anyone might be coming from the other direction and making enemies out of unspoken distrust of each other. While on his darkened porch Colonel Valerio drank *mate* in his shirt-sleeves, so many citizens were leaving town and their jobs, thanks to bricks thrown at all hours that cast up dust against the window panes, that over time others were able to get places for their sons behind the counter at the Post Office or land-office.

Other things, such as the hardships of winter and predictable sunsets in summer, remained pretty much unaffected by the men of the occupation.

Once, near the Christmas holidays of the first year, while she hovered over her husband with little plates of cheese, rolled-up salami, and slices of meat, the Colonel's wife breathed in deeply the odor of jasmine and remarked what a pity it was those flowers had so short a life.

Her man had a retort to that remark, and before taking a loud suck on his *mate*, said with the humor that always inspired her with security, "At the rate we are getting things under control, next year those jasmines will last three months."

On one of those same evenings, at the other end of town, Dina was in the kitchen chopping parsley when she realized the tango music coming across the gardens was breaking her heart.

The music was from the enormous Japanese boombox that Nacho Silvera owned three houses farther down the hill; the sound leapt in the window and swirled about various parts of her body, until she could no longer tell whether she was going through the beginning of euphoria or the end of deep sorrow.

It was as if she were reliving the December day she had left home to live with Black Johnny in his shack on the outskirts of Mosquitos. This contraption of Silvera's was turning loose from the patio under the medlar trees a fierce joy that mixed with her thoughts in the kitchen, turning them to the past. Parsley and hillbilly music intermingled with memories of her father holding a large microphone in his fist while he sang tangos for a children's school benefit.

Fated to live among singers, Dina knew an infinite number of tango verses, which she had learned from a notebook with corrugated cardboard covers that the old man kept squeezed under his left arm while he thrust the right into the air and sang until his throat dried out.

Between Nacho Silvera's house and the window frame, looking over the top of the primus burner, Dina could see a group of boys running like the devil behind a ball, and nearer to, inside the patio, was Johnny sitting behind the oleanders. Once in a while he would glance at the boys, but he remained rigid as a black statue, hands around the *mate* and his sight fixed on the recently watered seed beds.

While she listened to Silvera's music and at the same time watched Johnny with the blackened kettle between his *alpargatas* (rope sandals), she refused not to believe that Johnny, tough as a sea biscuit, should be doing better than singing in brothels in the guise of a solitary gringo. She was sure he would have had a better life if he had been willing to inherit that notebook her father had filled with a thousand sacrifices, saving himself a beginning singer's tedious work of gathering a repertoire. Too bad, she thought, there was no changing a Black like Johnny Sosa. A lot depended on upbringing, and if one was not as lucky as she had been, to grow up with tango in her blood, then life's sufferings were bound to flow from the heart into some other music.

Which was exactly what was happening to him, with the small addition that, when Johnny sang, only he understood the words. She knew that no one who frequented the Chanteclere, and perhaps no one in all of Mosquitos, with the exception of the priest Freire, understood English, if that was even the language in which Johnny sang.

Anyway, on the previous day, after having cleaned house at Doctor Fronte's, Dina had met up with the parish priest who was on his way back from exchanging novels at the Santanas' newsstand, and they spoke of the matter, with stentorian reproaches on the part of the priest. This encounter took place in the center of the plaza and very much against his will. It was plain it did not sit well with the priest to be seen talking out in the open with a woman who refused the sacrament and lived in concubinage.

"It's time your man stopped hanging out you know where," said the priest Freire, while tucking two war novels by Clark Carrados underneath a huge volume with black covers and gilt-edged pages.

She thought that if these words had come out of the mouth of any ordinary citizen, say the Lebanese haberdasher, she would simply have told him to go to hell and been on her way to her neighborhood on the hillside as usual on Thursdays. But she knew that to be on bad terms with the priest meant condemning herself to bad dreams every night. So she remained rooted like a plant before the priest, only daring to ask what Johnny was going to live on if he did not sing in brothels, because she too would be glad if he had opportunities somewhere else than the place he was frequenting out of necessity.

His face reddened by the wines of the widow Paroli, the priest thought about what Dina had said, and after a pause to pull himself together and briefly consult Providence, admitted he had been speaking of Johnny with Colonel Werner Valerio, when the subject had come up in a meeting of neighbors who intended once and for all to close every locale overrun with Brazilian women.

"Everyone agrees Johnny has a wonderful voice," the priest said. "But he ought to begin asking himself where will he be singing once that filthy place shuts down."

Like a benefactor extending a loser a second chance, he added that if Johnny were to sing in Spanish, the maestro Di Giorgio could take him on and arrange, when the time came, for his acceptance by an orchestra, his future assured.

"That would never happen to me," she said to Johnny when telling him of the encounter in the plaza. She was surprised that there still were people who concerned themselves about Johnny, even if it were only to recognize the merits of his voice. "If ever I am remembered it will be for *buñuelos* (deepfried cakes) at Doctor

Fronte's, because I won't ever have your luck. Take them up on it, and talk with this Di Giorgio to make yourself into a respectable singer."

When Johnny saw her crying as she had never cried before, he longed to be able by magic to change the course of their lives, because he was convinced that he would not find another woman like Dina if he were born anew, and that if he were to think well of himself, he'd have to take into account the opinion of one who had thrown in her lot with a loser.

Silent and confused, Johnny spent several days unable to make up his mind. He wandered around, restless, preparing a couple of new seed beds, one of peas and the other tall and rectangular, boarded up on four sides for small onions, although he thought in the midst of an immense yawn that he ought to prepare a third as well, for the uncertainty spreading inside him with the voracity of a weedy vine. Nor could he explain the roots of deep sorrow, thoughts he had never thought before that had to do with the question of how a Black man like himself had come to be what he was.

"What the hell must Melías Churi's life be like?" he wondered, while planting little onions a *jeme* apart. He thought about what would happen if the next day he were to get up early, set himself in the kitchen to look through the hole in the wall and then wait for seven o'clock to turn on the two-battery radio. But he knew at this time of year the magical mists would not be appearing in the chink, and he'd only be disappointed. All he might accomplish, he'd say to himself, was to learn who the traitor was who had taken the place of the man of *The Fertile Hour in the Early Dawn*, some obscure personage who never would have as fantastic a story to tell as that of the great one from Austin, of which only he, Johnny, knew the ending. "Maybe there is no one at that hour," he thought. "Maybe it is forbidden to talk on the air at seven in the morning, because soldiers can't be bothered to police announcers that early."

He was feeling miserable, without direction, and what was worse, about to lose the little he had accomplished on his own as a singer. He, a Black man with no education, like Lou Brakley, had taken on the hardest tasks, the lowest wages, and made all the sacrifices necessary in order to talk to other failures about how hard his past had been. But musing just then on a Friday evening when he had finished watering seed beds, he was no longer so sure.

As he sat on the little stool behind the oleanders, looking without seeing what he had been doing, he knew that behind him, through the open window, Dina's eyes were boring a hole in the back of his neck, exasperated at having to wait for him to make up his mind once in his life. He could also hear the ruckus of that cursed Japanese boombox, set at full volume three shacks farther down by Nacho Silvera's wife, a feverish mulatto capable of dancing in her sleep.

"Those damned Blacks don't let me think," he complained, knowing it was one more excuse to put off a little longer an inevitably bitter decision.

"How lovely Nacho's set must be," came from a neck through the window announcing time was up.

"The guy must be a prick," he said, cross because he did not appreciate the way Dina was foisting change on him. She'd surely think differently if she'd seen him even once on the platform at the Chanteclere, bent over the light on the strings, the Black Diamond like an automatic rifle pointed at Nazis who refuse to understand. And yet everyone did understand him, he was thinking. He struck them in the heart, and elsewhere.

"But times change and the light goes out," he said to himself with a sigh of surrender, getting up and going *mate* in hand toward the kitchen window. Dina turned innocent, her head bent over the parsley-chopping, concentrated on her small felled forests.

"All right," said Johnny. "I'll talk to maestro Di Giorgio, although I don't know what it is he'll do with me."

She looked at him, her eyes very bright, as if to say, "My poor dear Black, what a way to cut through thorns and tree stumps," but said nothing. She let him go to the bedroom to dress all in black, put on the silver medallion, and start down the hill in his usual long strides toward the house the priest had indicated. As he left, Johnny had that alert look in the eye of someone thinking, "I'm going, but I am not getting screwed."

Yet without saying it in so many words, he was screwed. How to tamp his desire to be what he wanted to be was planned casually during leisure moments by the gathering of notables who had pledged themselves to his transformation, a scheme Johnny discovered too late.

The first steps occurred by chance that very night—although by then no one in Mosquitos thought anything happened by chance— as they silently waited for the old man to reveal his plans for remaking Johnny.

Maestro Di Giorgio was an elderly tenor of well-known lineage, a long history of misanthropy, and an acid expression on his face, who had been looking for the last hidden corner on earth, so long as it contained a billiard table and cultivated people open to astonishment at his erudition.

He thought he'd located that spot in Mosquitos, then realized that the town's few cultured persons did not cross paths with the loafers of the Euskalduna bar, the only place in the whole town where such a green felt table was to be found. Thus the Italian maestro resolved to patronize the grill at Doctor Fronte's house, gossip with Colonel Valerio when he appeared on the scene, and dazzle both with his learning. He could talk about La Scala of Milan the way Johnny Sosa did of the Chanteclere. No one enjoyed these conversations more than the priest Freire—stories about musical popes with a double life, or the exemplary careers of Carlo De Luca, Fiorello Vastías, or Gironella, men who had triumphed on the European stage thanks to maestro Di Giorgio, who after long months of work, had taught them to pronounce magisterially the dark *u* in the middle of a song.

Johnny had been standing under the grapevine since early evening waiting for the anecdotes to finish and felt considerably relieved when the old singing master, by the light of a lamp in Doctor Fronte's patio, glanced admiringly at his tonsils and assured him that, if he followed his advice step by step, Colonel Valerio might arrange for him to attend the Coast to Coast

Festival, and, uncontaminated by the usual self-promotion of the stars, represent the little town of Mosquitos with his singing.

Engulfed in the smoke from the sausages the colonel was turning over and over with the point of a bayonet, Johnny stood astonished by the proposal. While he thought it over, and the rest swirled the ice around in their amber glasses, the singing master was explaining to Doctor Fronte—a man always in a vest, incapable of saying no, and whom many took for a fool—about the manner in which Toscanini recruited his unknown musicians.

"The great master," he said with the expansive gestures of a preacher, "went to wakes, just to listen to the bands that played on Sunday in the plaza—drunks, men out of work, Bohemian rabble of the worst sort—where Toscanini singled out his pupils and changed them into the artistic geniuses of the era." And looking at Johnny crouched, almost invisibly in a corner of the patio where the light hardly reached, he added, "So I can do the same with you, boy."

With an absent air, as if he wanted to be alone, the Colonel settled himself with a large scotch before going back to the grill. Over the top of his glass, his attention was caught by a sparkle from the medallion that hung from Johnny's neck; he watched Johnny straining, but said nothing. Then back at the grill, the Colonel slapped the back of the priest Freire, who was enduring the pain of an empty stomach by bending over with his knees wide apart and his cassock making a hanging bridge, and said good-naturedly, "Reverend, I think these sausages are done."

Johnny realized that no one would begin eating as long as he was present. He'd have to say something convincing before he went or before Doctor Fronte had a whimsical thought, like sending him to scrub the patio in the dark or fetch a block of ice from the bar.

"Well, I'm leaving," he said abruptly.

"You're leaving?" said the Colonel, while he made a longitudinal cut in a still sizzling sausage.

"Yes," Johnny answered, neither soft nor loud.

"Yes sir, you say," the Colonel corrected.

"Yes sir," Johnny said again.

But he did not mind saying it. On the contrary, he was so strangely seduced by the officer's tone of voice, that if the man had been drunk and somewhere else, Johnny might well have answered in English. For he was reminded of the calm, firm tone of a commander he had seen in *Fort Laramie* one very hot afternoon. While dreading the final deadly siege by a band of Cheyenne sons-of-bitches, the old officer gave out a declamatory, unquestionably heroic order that brought a sharp "iés, séar!" from the captain, a man with lips parched from thirst, a true hero obliged to obey to the letter this bullying from the strong, on a night just as dark as the impulse that had sent Johnny's thoughts so far afield.

"Well, boy, where are we?" asked the maestro. "Do you like the idea of singing in Castilian and smiling like a normal singer?"

Johnny looked at him suspiciously. No one in Mosquitos thought Johnny standoffish—if he didn't give out a broad smile in friendly greeting, it was simply because he had no teeth. Not even bad teeth, because to say that, he'd have to have *some*. Ever since his teeth had loosened like stakes and left to smile elsewhere, Johnny's gums had been as smooth as a good Roman Catholic's knees.

Maestro Di Giorgio guessed what made him hesitate, and said, "I know what you are thinking, boy. You'll have to get those missing teeth before you come to my house for singing lessons. You will start very humbly, from zero."

The Colonel was making fantastic noises in his throat while he ate. "Which do you like best, bolero or tango music?" he asked.

It seemed incredible to Johnny that a man of war should ask him about music. Actually, he did not care for either kind, but if he told the truth, that what he liked was the blues and the bluer the better and had no mind to change preferences, they would get upset, and worse, leave him with nothing. "His teeth were the windows of his soul," Melías Churi liked to say in *The Fertile Hour in the Early Dawn*, referring to the effect of Lou Brakley's smile when he clinched a friendship.

"The bolero," Johnny said.

"I thought you'd say that," the Colonel smiled without ceasing to chew with his mouth open. "Tomorrow you go to the barracks and tell the dentist you are Colonel Valerio's singer. He'll see to you."

Doctor Fronte was the only one capable of making out Johnny's true thoughts, but he kept his conclusions to himself, the fruit of considerable knowledge of the people in the small town, intimacies that not even the priest Freire was allowed to hear in the shadows of the confessional. He knew the Black was telling barefaced lies, but could not think what was keeping him from saying what, on any other occasion, he gladly would have said—that boleros were for queers who fancied lyric poetry. To know that Johnny was torn in indecision irritated Fronte, at the same time as the gentle agree-ableness of the alcohol was softening him enough to wonder whether life had brutalized Blacks like the case before him so badly they felt emotions only weakly.

"That's right," Doctor Fronte announced suddenly, pointing a finger at Johnny's chest. "We'll set you up in good shape, but the brothel performances are over."

Johnny could not rely on the firmness of his voice and said nothing.

"So you like bolero, *ché*," remarked the Colonel, lowering the corners of his mouth, as if Doctor Fronte had not spoken. "What do you say we send the crazy ladies back to Brazil, and give Mosquitos a star singer?"

Freire emptied a china pitcher into the men's glasses and began talking of the glorious scandals the priest José Mujica had caused in Mexico in the fifties when he'd get down from the altar to sing love songs.

Grasping the Belgian bayonet the better to emphasize his words, the Colonel declared that a good example, and observed that Father Mujica, in the midst of spiritual tortures, finally had had to hang up his cassock in order to go on singing. He furthermore added that he knew many cases in history of people who had had to give up something before the alternative of unreconcilable passions, for if they had tried to live with both, the one inevitably would ruin the other.

"In the end, the victim, with glazed eyes, walks to

the slaughterhouse without anyone's having to force him," he said.

Outside all was still, one of those small-town silences in which only the dull sound of night insects smashing against the lamps vibrates in the ear of anyone consciously listening.

The three men continued talking of other arcane subjects and so decidedly ignored the presence of the fourth person that Johnny took it as a dismissal and found himself shutting the patio gate and his feet on the sidewalk.

Next to the curb, a couple of soldiers smoking and talking in incredibly low voices inside a jeep watched him standing there a moment, paralyzed, so angry that at first he could not decide in which direction his steps should take him.

For a while they were quiet in the shadows, but as Johnny did not move, one of the soldiers got down from the vehicle with an ostentatious rattling of metals, got close enough to Johnny to smell him, and took firm hold of his shoulder.

"Keep going, brother," he said. "Because if the Colonel finds you standing here, he'll hang you up by your balls."

"Like the priest José Mujica," Johnny said, without knowing quite why he said it. He shrugged the fellow off for trying to jerk him around and obligingly took off for the faithful darkness of the little town, where it was possible to lose himself in the wealth of honeysuckle and not have to listen to any such advice from anyone.

*V*ISIBLY IRRITATED, THE SOLDIER SAW HIM COMING, his eyes concealed in the depths of a helmet as enormous and black as a stew kettle, and when Johnny was only a few steps away, and the soldier was certain that the approaching man had no intention of slowing down, he stopped him cold in front of the dwarfs posted at the entrance.

Waving his weapon to keep the good-for-nothing from depositing himself on top of the saddest of the dwarfs, the guard asked, without lowering the bayonet attached to his gun, what the devil made him think a Black could go wandering into a military compound during a state of siege.

Johnny glanced up quickly to see the hollow-cheeked face secreted within the helmet. "Cool it, Gutiérrez," he said, his voice firm and low, and deliberately sat himself down on the head of the nearest dwarf. "The dentist is expecting me. Go and tell him the Colonel's singer is here."

The hidden face turned to him and, convinced that Johnny Sosa's impertinence was not an illusion, said to another guard, "Look, corporal, that Black over there says the dentist is expecting him and that he was sent by Colonel Valerio. How do we know it's true?"

A third soldier picked up the message, took his time to disappear among the varnished barracks, and half an hour later the chain of olive-green suits retraced its path.

The answer surprised Johnny, whose eyes had been meandering over town's first dwellings. From this spot, where it had never before occurred to him to observe them, he saw situated lower down among the rocks and stones a tortuous row of scattered shanties, each of straw and corrugated tin, looking from that height too fragile to be of the least significance.

When the soldier grudgingly reported that permission was granted for him to enter, Johnny walked past with his head down. Fingering the medallion on his chest, he prayed that nobody from the hillside hamlet was watching to see him, on his own, cross over the terrible red and white barrier flanked by the dentist's dwarfs.

And thus, inconspicuously and trivially, commenced what would turn out to be the beginning of the end.

During the following days, even though Johnny turned mute and fled from encounters with anyone he recognized, the priest Freire, the Colonel, maestro Di Giorgio, and the guards, everyone knew of the orthodontic work in progress and the kidney-shaped mouth gagging in pink paste in preparation for a smile never seen before.

At last, one morning with appropriate drizzle and terrible weather, rigid as a post in the dentist's chair with his fingers clasped over his belly, Johnny saw the results of the numerous engineering efforts.

"Cheer up boy, I am about to install your chops," said the dentist. He was a large man of domineering character who from the start had looked to Johnny exactly like Burl Ives in *Green Hell*. The man was endowed with that hidden concern doctors display after being submerged for years in the depths of the tropics, and which generally blossoms when they have to face naked Blacks before a mass vaccination.

So he opened his mouth wide, feeling he was providing the hole for *tejo* players to toss stones into (or his dreams of the future), and allowed the entrance of that immaculately smooth, pink and perfect mold that abruptly filled the cavity with teeth white as milk.

"Incredible," said the man, holding up Johnny's lip to a magnifying mirror.

Johnny could see they really were beautiful, but so overpowering that when it came time to take leave of the guards, he had to stretch a mouth that threatened to freeze for the rest of his days into an expression of astonishment, as involuntary and contorted as a horse's yawn.

At home, Dina was ripping apart an old shirt for dish towels, and when she saw Johnny enter the patio, his lips thicker than usual and sealed shut as if he resolved to keep permanent silence, she knew she was faced with a new man. Setting the rags aside, she tickled his ribs to force a smile out of him, and then hugged him hard, with the secret intention he should nibble her ear or the scruff of her neck, as she had seen in passionate scenes on the screen at the Daguerre, and never, until this nasty rainy day, had had the possibility of duplicating.

Dina sensed that something even more important than teeth had changed, and without knowing why, without knowing how to say it, she dragged Johnny to the bed, loosened his belt and soon both were naked, in black and white, mute under the dripping sky, and fucking at high noon. She was feverish, accommodating her body in as many ways as she could for him to imprint fresh nibbles on her buttocks, her lips, on the skin of her back, on her tongue, and finally bite into the rock-hard crackers she brought for afterwards, which Johnny, splayed out over the head of the bed, ground mercilessly to the last crumb.

She watched him in silence. She thought it good to be looking at the complete male, and it occurred to her that Nacho Silvera must have felt equally powerful before his woman the day he showed up holding in both hands his enormous Japanese tape recorder, to have his own dance music whenever he wanted it.

"Sing for me," she said, and in the same impulse flew out from the sheets, returning with the bathroom mirror in one hand and the guitar in the other.

And Johnny sang. He wrinkled his brow as though he were taking on far away sorrows and practiced new facial expressions reflected intact from the mirror she had propped on his belly, and then an expression of complete contentment came over him.

"You crazy Black," she murmured, shaken, watching him move his head as if in beautiful doubt. His fingers rose and fell over the guitar strings, while his muscles shone with the fervor of someone leaning back exhausted against a dry adobe wall. Then Johnny began, without the least sign of a smile, the very dark, slow, and unintelligible cadences of *"No hay fantasmas"* ("There

Are No Ghosts,") trying to make her feel those verses sinking one by one into her bones, just as he always had sung them in a lugubrious melancholy strumming that went back to the plantations of the Mississippi and had been brought on a glorious Saturday to the Daguerre by that sweet and wayward Tammy, in order that he, in his genius, could make them his own and drive mad the gullible girls of the Chanteclere.

But Dina responded quite differently. Naked and white, kneeling and perched on her heels, moving to the liquid beat of Johnny's rhythm, she held the mirror and watched his teeth barely insinuated in his gums, especially when he lifted his chin toward the ceiling and moaned almost at the end, "*Ay, ay, ay, fantasma de novela, sube y no ceses de subir*" ("Storied ghost, rise and do not cease to rise"), she felt all the more convinced that she had done well to encourage him to give up a life that, as hard he might try, would never bring him out to the light of day.

But when Johnny had finished, and they were left looking eye to eye from either end of the bed as though glancing across an imaginary auditorium, he needed no words to know that argument was useless, that there was something vaguely fraudulent in it all, and that he was beginning to care for Dina less.

"What do you think they will do with me?" he said, slowly setting the guitar aside and not waiting for an answer.

She did not know either. What she did know was that, from the moment Johnny returned from the barracks and entered the patio in the drizzle, when they entwined their legs in bed and he had sung and done it all without giving her a single real smile, a true despair had begun to flower within her.

F OR SOME TIME JOHNNY HAD BEEN SUFFERING SOUL-wrenching torments, not at all clear about whether those claiming to lead him by the hand to triumph were looking after him as a younger son or as a race horse.

But while he judged it prudent not to ask himself too many questions before he followed to the letter the advice intended to change him into the new man of Mosquitos, the fact that he might be auctioning off a recent past charged with scenes impeccably acted out as quick as a heartbeat shook him to the core, and there was nothing on the horizon to make him suppose that his life was going to become any less terrible than before.

He'd feel crazed with shame on Saturday nights when certain objects seemed to come to life—the bone comb, the boots shoved under the bed, or the medallion of the mariners' saint, each ready for another brilliant performance at the Chanteclere.

"We've been waiting for you, gaucho," María Teresa de Australia would be saying, looking exaggeratedly anxious at her little gold watch.

And Johnny, all in silver and black, would step onto the platform and sing, while Tomé Cara de Humo hopped like a rabbit among the tables dispensing bottles from his aluminum tray.

Such thoughts came to him regularly on each trip to and from classes with maestro Di Giorgio. They worked on him like thick eucalyptus bark, sending him inside himself, and he planned his route so as to avoid his meeting up in the plaza with anyone he knew from the brothel or noticing that the town was as empty at night as in the times of yellow fever.

On just two occasions did his eyes open up to what was going on outside him, and if the third time is the charm, that happened some time later, almost without his being aware of the order of events.

The first came on a chance meeting with the priest

Freire, who was coming back at the siesta hour from exchanging detective stories, and asked how singing classes were going.

Johnny felt nervous because he had never conversed with the priest out in the street before, and while he was telling him, trying not to let anger show, that the last exercise had been about learning to breathe and walk at the same time, for as long as the encounter lasted he could not stop turning over and over the medallion hanging from his neck.

"Don't fiddle with the saint, boy," the priest said. "It's time you stood on your own two feet and stopped running to your saint for every little thing."

The second time was the afternoon he was on his way to the maestro's house to begin singing melodies with a carpenter's pencil between his teeth, having finished with the breathing exercises.

Although he only knew the rest of the teachers at the elementary school by sight, to run into elderly Erminia the way he did affected him as it might a person who, after not seeing a loved one for a long time, suddenly met up with him boxed in his coffin at a wake.

Put off guard by the siesta quiet, he ran right into a gigantic military operation that was cordoning off the large old house where the town's three teachers lived. Dogs on leashes flanked Colonel Valerio, who was entering the house, shirt sleeves rolled up and pistol in hand. While who knows what went on inside, a canvas-topped pickup made its way through the shoulder-to-shoulder guard that had closed off the street and parked before the geraniums at the front gate, allowing a dozen men to get down and disperse among the garden plantings.

Pretty soon the militia emerged again at a trot, hurrying along the three women with their heads covered, in such a manner that Johnny was not able to tell which was the principal Erminia, the organizer of memorable school benefits during the Korean War, in which Dina's now deceased father had taken part, singing tangos into the silver microphone.

With his back turned, sorting out musical scores at the dining room table, Maestro Di Giorgio listened to Johnny's account of the incident.

When he turned around, he had a stern expression Johnny had not seen before, and said to him, "Look boy, I know you're upset," and spoke briefly about the times when Italy had been through similar situations and how a cautious man like himself had come out safe from such a hell. Those women must have done something to bring on what Johnny had seen from the front walk, he said, but that should not distract him from his work toward a place one day in the Coast to Coast Festival.

Then the man handed him the score with the title, *Bésame Mucho*, printed in huge characters, and after tapping their heels against the tiles, they began to sing.

Hours later, facing a plate of lentils at dinner, Johnny remarked to Dina how Erminia had been taken away from the teachers' house.

"There must be a reason," said she without batting an eye. "You just keep on going, knowing good luck is in your favor, even though there may be things we hear about and do not understand."

"I did not hear about it, woman," Johnny protested, "I saw it."

She said she was not actually referring to that. She was thinking about how that same morning she had not understood exactly what Doctor Fronte meant when she was cleaning weeds out of the flower pots and he had come out to the patio in his underwear, watching her work while he scratched his belly.

"In a few years you will have me to thank for not having to be a servant around here any longer," he had said to her, all the while eyeing her rear as she crouched to clean the plants. "But first we will have the black Phoenix rising from the ashes."

"How nice," she had said, paying him with a timid smile that had all the signs of deference.

Nevertheless, she was left unable to decipher the meaning of the words, because Doctor Fronte then went inside on the excuse of washing his face before his wife got up.

"That was what I was referring to," said Dina while washing dinner plates in the brass bowl. But she might as well have thought it all to herself, because Johnny had gone quietly to the patio and was beneath the stars, asking himself if the business of putting his fate into the hands of experts was as good an idea as it was cracked up to be.

*J*OHNNY SQUINTED THROUGH THE CHINK IN THE ADOBE wall and saw her coming like Dorothy Malone's entering from the side of the screen at the Daguerre, when in *The Last Sunset (El ultimo atardecer)* she had walked to the stable with a bucket of water for the horses and came upon Kirk Douglas on his back in the hay, caught in the act of unbuttoning her own daughter's blouse, an image of normality jolted by surprise. Dina, back from morning clean-up at Doctor Fronte's, had stopped, slow and dazed, to watch, with the same alarm as Dorothy Malone and the neighbors, the way Nacho's children were running up dangerously close to the soldiers, then quickly back again, and falling back behind the tomato plants crying. Not out of fear, Johnny thought in open admiration behind the crack, more likely from the tremendous courage it took to go so close and taunt them. The children's voices, sharp, angry, and wild, came and went on a shaky breeze that mixed noises with the wood smoke brushing off straw roofs, and made a sorrowful complaint against injustice and on behalf of the man missing.

Until that Saturday noon Johnny had thought differently about Nacho Silvera—a giant glad-hander too big for his bicycle, hardly the spectacular puppeteer he had bragged of becoming. Johnny had been convinced that for Nacho the world was just about right as it was, and change would not set too well with him, because if it came about, Nacho let it be known, he would no longer be allowed to dream the impossible.

Nervously rubbing the *mate* between his hands, Johnny thought that Nacho Silvera really was just a seller of bread and sausages, someone any neighbor would have suspected had his dreams fulfilled the moment he installed that Japanese boombox with those speakers that could shake figs off trees three blocks away. Just that. Nacho asked no more of life than to sell enough sausages to allow him to sit entire nights with a clear conscience, listening to Caribbean stations without anyone nagging him that there weren't enough beans in the family stew pot.

Little as he knew him, his few glimpses had drawn from Johnny a lasting respect that grew whenever he spotted that steaming three-wheeled cart on the sidewalk on its way to the Chanteclere.

Perhaps because they had never had the opportunity to raise a glass alone together at a table in the bar, or because the sausage vendor didn't like embittered persons and tellers of sentimental stories, Johnny was left unaware of the depth of those plans in which he was himself invariably included with the same theatrical line, the same supercilious smile: "Black, with your looks and my nerve, there must be a future for the two of us on this planet."

But it was enough for the presence of a third intruder, like Terelú, who would drag her whiny self into the middle of the conversation to ask over and over if there was going to be room for prostitutes in heaven, for the stone giant to lose his temper and leave the bar running so fast his heels smacked the back of his neck.

And so, putting it off for another time, he'd interrupt his old dream of touring America with puppet shows of smiling dolls made of gourds that would tell the story of Mosquitos, one that was seeming to become more complicated and tortuous all the time, as Nacho kept adding stories stolen from the towns he intended to leave behind.

"Buenos Aires will be the first!" he'd shout from the sidewalk, mounted on his half-bicycle attached to the cart, a strange and colorful invention that hid in its interior a lighted primus stove and a frying pan where sausages sizzled.

Then he'd disappear, stiff in the darkness, to pedal for a couple of hours through the gas-lit streets and at last stop in front of the door of the Daguerre to sell the rest of his wares before the movie finished.

But on Thursday night Nacho went out as usual, pedaling the heavy cart-full, left the vehicle to one side of the plaza, and disappeared from town, depriving his wife and four children of any explanation for his abandonment.

But what had been a mystery all that night and on the following day was cleared up at noon on Saturday, when, in the middle of serious kitchen activities—stews simmering and men with a brick scrubbing at the filth around their necks—suddenly a contingent of armed soldiers in full cry surrounded the Silvera family's shanty.

Stepping on the heads of various chickens in the way, the men in green kicked open the front Dutch door and then, from his outpost in the kitchen, Johnny could see them come out with Nacho's giant apparatus, his wife trotting behind them, waving her arms in useless protest.

Just as Dina entered her own door, the soldiers were making the sausage vendor's wife get into the back of an old Power Wagon, then lowered the canvas cover and left for whence they had come, while the children's terrified cries swelled after the vehicle.

"What could he have done that's so unusal?" Johnny asked, making the dentures click against his palate.

Flushed from the effort of the climb, Dina set a basin with soapy water down in front of her chair and submerged her reddened feet. With a sigh of relief, she raised her blue eyes to see Johnny's puzzled look of regret for all he had not been able to see clearly.

"What's wrong with you?" she said.

"What do you mean what's wrong with me? With me, nothing," Johnny said. He was speaking gruffly, hesitatingly. "I was only asking what Nacho could have done for all this to be happening at his house."

"Nothing's happened to him, because he made himself scarce. It was the Japanese boombox. The one he has . . . had. They say he only got it to listen to short wave stations, and that is not allowed," she explained gloomily, anger surrounding her words. She kept to herself the genuine weariness she had been feeling walking up the hill, as that Saturday was the last evening she'd be opening the kitchen window and remembering times when her father had been an interesting man, constructing for herself a good and colorful past while she prepared dinner and listened to the deafening program of tango music the stone giant was providing three shanties away.

But at the same time she had the uncomfortable feeling of having been let down in her good faith, made victim of a low deception. That beautiful artifact that for months had charmed her from a distance was after all no more than a six-battery delinquent, flaunting implausible sounds and glittering images, able to make a legion of gypsies lose their sense of reality.

"So he can go to hell," she concluded, scrubbing her toes hard with a pumice stone.

"What do you mean he can go to hell?" Johnny said surprised. "What is wrong with listening to short wave?"

"What's wrong with it?" she mimicked. "It's wrong because on short wave there is talk against the government."

"Who talks?" Johnny asked, regretting for the first time the limitations of his single-wave Spika.

"They, the Russians," Dina said. Then she took her feet out of the tub and put them, still wet, into her *alpargatas*.

There came to Johnny's mind a French dairy farmer of the Resistance he had seen in a film at the Daguerre. Every night, while the family was resting, the fellow took a lantern to the shed where the cows slept and between the bags of feed, nervous and impatient, he connected the hidden parts of a radio, in the hope of listening to coded transmissions of the Normandy landing.

The night the signal was sent, almost at the end of the movie, that peasant in waistcoat and gaiters had fallen into a merry drunk and was surprised by two Germans as he slept under a cow with the blaring radio playing London's latest musical hits.

Johnny felt only deep respect for the fugitive sausage vendor, because it occurred to him that if in place of the French dairy farmer it had been Nacho Silvera who was awaiting the signal of the Normandy landings, the Germans would have passed by that farm and not captured anyone, as Nacho, to judge by the incidents of the last days, had shown himself to be less slack-jawed than the Frenchman.

And so Johnny remained silent, filling the kitchen with his generous humanity, his eyes glued on Dina's feet, her naked toes outlined in the damp cloth of her *alpargatas*.

Dina poured alcohol into the primus to begin cooking and commented that it would be useless for Nacho to try to escape because, sooner or later, the military were going to catch him wherever he might be.

Johnny thought the last word was yet to be said, hope coming to him from his own wild imagination, from his memory of those Frenchmen marching through the swamps and going right past the Germans.

When he went out to the patio he stood for a long time looking at the silenced shanty of the Silveras. The children were nowhere to be seen. Nacho must have been a long way off by then, in Buenos Aires perhaps. He could imagine him trying to convince a businessman with a bad shave that his puppets were worth seeing anywhere on the planet.

Then he kicked at one of the empty carnation pots and asked himself who in this story would play the French.

A FEW DAYS AFTER THE INCIDENT AT THE SILVERAS', Colonel Werner Valerio was in his office in the barracks going through dossiers on private individuals, when an investigative officer arrived to tell him that the singer Johnny Sosa in his opinion had taken his first misstep.

The Colonel motioned the man to a seat in the corner, next to the window that looked out onto eucalyptus trees, and for a good while continued leafing through the newly completed secret file that referred to the priest Bartolomé Freire.

While the other stared into the trees, the Colonel reflected bitterly that if his military service in this spot where civil authorities previously worked gave him anything, it was the constant surprise about the vast distance within the human soul between its well cultivated surface and its deformed depths. Other than that, he was thinking, who would have suspected that in the private library of a man like the priest Freire, far from finding a single book related to the understanding of theology and spiritual phenomena, there reposed the greatest variety of works of pornographic entertainment he had ever come across in his life in army quarters?

Wall to wall in the priest's hallowed seat, there extended, according to the series of reports, the obscene editions of *Tit-bits*, the three apocryphal Chilean versions of *The Russian Princess*, the eleven volumes of the dictionary of the terror of Vergara Mercado, the embarassing "Apologia for the Prick" by the author of the national anthem, and innumerable titles of obvious sentimental attraction, such as *The Queen of the Valley*, the first western novel written by Marcial Lafuente Estefanía, from the twenties.

"Now I no longer believe even in the peace of the grave," Colonel Valerio said, disgusted. He slammed shut the file and put it in the bottom drawer of his desk, wondering how he was going to react the next time he met the priest.

He stood observing the tops of the eucalyptus trees. A flock of magpies was making a great racket in a nest that was too small. The Colonel shook off his fatigue, lowered his eyes, and asked the man in the chair what all this was about a misstep taken by Johnny Sosa.

That individual wrinkled the bristly whiskers on his upper lip and stood up, reporting that the singer he had been assigned to watch had gone out very early from his shanty on the hillside to spend the morning in the Euskalduna bar, where he had made some odd remarks in front of the customers.

The Colonel's expression was between pain and collapse, and he went back to looking at the magpies. He said to himself that if those birds were better managed, they might learn to widen the nest at the sides and not toward the bottom as they were doing.

"Odd remarks?" he asked without taking his eyes off the tree tops. "What odd remarks?"

It was a fact. "I am not going back to old Di Giorgio," were the exact words, spoken in a loud voice in the Euskalduna bar on the plaza, while he sprinkled pinches of salt on one of the hard-boiled eggs that the Basque always kept in the impeccable glass bell jar, provided for nausea from the first cane drink of the morning.

Of the characters who were leaning on the bar—two dark men given over to early sorrows, a road inspector discontented for lack of a future, the dairyman Romeo Toss, who religiously every Wednesday walked to the center of Mosquitos hoping that would be the day his dear son were set free, or the man under the twirled mustache—not one paid the least attention to the remarks, not even to say to Johnny, "That's your affair, brother."

From Johnny's point of view, it would have been ideal if the whole town, people of all ages, friends and enemies, brothel women and well-known policemen had all been there, crowded into the deserted bar room just to witness the decision he had come to, but not say anything on the subject afterwards.

"I am not going to old Di Giorgio any more, Basque," he repeated again, highly pleased.

One could see in him the profound satisfaction of evolving a design, a plan, that transcendent moment of enchantment that shines only on those who, at a moment of seemingly no importance—in the middle of a walk to nowhere in particular, or while breaking a dead twig, or stretching the left arm into the sleeve of a checkered jacket—release into the open air the faculty to defy all existence. To decide, if it suits them, that for all the storm clouds that may be hovering in the sky in the morning, it is not going to rain.

The Basque Euskalduna was not surprised that Johnny, who never had sung two songs alike, did not have it in him to learn anything new. He had watched his growing up from when he was a lump of chocolate on his way to school, and knew his work habits had not progressed beyond selling caged chickens or apples he'd picked off the ground in the plaza fair. At least since he'd been singing in the Chanteclere on Saturday nights, the Basque gave him credit that the wages he gathered in that quince jelly tin were enough to keep any gossip from saying he lived off his woman, the blonde Dina. But the bar owner thought less of him when he learned that Johnny Sosa, in the hands of maestro Di Giorgio and others of Colonel Valerio's lackeys, had now given up that modest life to emulate the careers of Lucho Gatica or Antonio Prieto, and would be entering the Coast to Coast festival with triumphs arranged ahead of time.

"Singing second-hand songs is not going to get him anywhere," the Basque had declared at the time. "Johnny will be ruined and crooning like any other Black in the band."

"Pretty soon we'll see him in work clothes hoeing the officers' gardens," said the regulars.

"I can see him running errands for the Colonel's wife," said others.

"One day he is going to give himself away, be staked out, have the shit beaten out of him, his woman taken away, and then it will be all over for the Black," the Basque said.

Which was why, on hearing the line repeated twice about giving up bolero classes with old Di Giorgio, the Basque Euskalduna glanced up to where Johnny was peeling another egg and shrugged his shoulders.

"There is going to be trouble," was all he could think to say.

"That was all the Basque bartender said," reported the officer of the bushy whiskers, lowering his voice and watching through the windows the wild racket of the magpies.

"And the Black, what did he say?" the Colonel asked.

"Nothing. He did not say anything. He laughed is all, showed the new teeth we gave him and left the bar eating his hard-boiled egg. And that was the end of it, Colonel," said the other, still gazing outside. It was evident he was toying with a violent notion regarding the eucalyptus, the magpies, and the mess of twigs they were making on the military patio.

"And what do you think of it all?" Colonel Valerio went on to ask.

The other, caught by surprise, brought his eyes back to the desk.

"I think it is wrong, Colonel," he said straightening up in his hair. "I think one should be more grateful toward those who do something for one, because, for instance, if someone had made me a present of teeth like for this Black traitor, which I could certainly use, especially in back, I would not be ashamed to go around saying, wherever appropriate, thanks to you with these teeth I can chew crackers and even tiles. But you know, my Colonel, how those Blacks are, because I'm telling you, if it had been me—"

"Pity you can't sing," the Colonel cut him off.

*C*ATCHING SIGHT OF HIM FRAMED IN THE DOORWAY, and suddenly appearing like a bad statue out of place, Tomé Cara de Humo ducked his head and activated his cleaning rag, dusting beer bottles and wiping up puddles on the bar counter. True, he was glad to see that figure all in black, his large silver medallion and majestic solitude. But he knew if Johnny stepped over the door frame, he'd be as foolhardy to enter as a bird lured by bird feed, and worse, he'd be the excuse that they were waiting for—a Saturday here—a Sunday there, to close the Chanteclere for good. So he prayed that no one had seen him yet, that the fool would think twice, turn around, and get lost in the night without violating the prohibition imposed on him when he was given his teeth.

But Terelú saw him.

Wrapped in a Portuguese shawl, her fists buried in the cloudy depths of her breasts, she said, her voice cold, "Don't come in, Johnny." She said it as had Tomé Cara de Humo, knowing the Chanteclere was doomed if he came in, letting her fears sink to the bottom of the vermouth glass in front of her, in the hope that when she raised her big black eyes again, Johnny Sosa would have disappeared thanks to one more miracle of the brothel saint.

"Come on in, country boy," Celeste said maliciously to herself, being among those who assumed the Black had sold out cheap and willingly installed himself under the wing of the aging pimp of a maestro, Abraham Di Giorgio.

"Stay where you are, love. Go home," begged María Teresa de Australia, knowing Johnny's compulsion toward doom.

But as much as they might be divided between two desires, everyone fixed their attention on the pair of sparkling boots in the doorway, long enough for the new arrival to glance over the hall like someone who, after many years, wants to look inside his childhood home.

Then, hands deep in his pockets, Johnny took the first step and entered. Then he took the second and third steps, picked a careful path among the tables, slowly took out of the pocket the hand he greeted with to wave away cigarette smoke, and by dint of some impeccable teeth capable of inspiring terror amid the deepest sorrow, completed his entrance with the gift of a glorious smile.

"*Opa*, Johnny," said one of the post office clerks, mischievously pointing his chin toward the footstool covered with old newspapers, on which still sat the quince jelly tin for honoraria.

"It's all right, old man" said Johnny while he massaged an invisible gum. When he reached the bar, the regulars leaning against the counter opened a space for him, and he held his hands out palms up toward Tomé Cara de Humo, in a greeting somewhere between friendly and triumphant, as he'd seen in movies that showed Blacks working in the Bronx. The waiter grudgingly slapped those palms twice with his, and Johnny laughed broadly, making visible a well aligned double row of molars in the back.

"How are you, Tomé. It's not so warm in here anymore, like the other guy said," the Black greeted him.

"Just so, Johnny, we do our duty," said the bartender, serving him a beer. Terelú moved closer and squeezed his shoulder affectionately, but without saying anything. Celeste also moved up and on the way let drip sweet treachery.

"The Colonel gave you permission to stay up late?" came out between her teeth.

"Thanks, girl. No need to sweeten the broth," Johnny said and forgot about her for the rest of the night. But he could sense hostility, a grayness, changes in the night. He put down his beer quietly and spent some time looking at the empty shelves, the too-still curtain to the back room through which the women used to come and go, the tables more like Tuesday than Saturday night, and new groups of people, mixed races from the north, "military in civvies," he thought to himself.

"The say they are going to close the Chanteclere," Terelú said in a low voice, reproach coloring her words and giving him to understand that many things had changed since he had abandoned the brothel to learn boleros and other melodies from the enemy.

Johnny shrugged his shoulders, but not disrespectfully. He said he did not see how the Chanteclere was going to save itself from the same inexplicable fate as Melías Churi, the teacher Erminia and the other teachers, the son of Romeo Toss, as who knows how many others who went to bed one night and the next day were gone, as Nacho Silvera's Japanese boombox and his wife, for all that it made him glad, Johnny said, that the sausage vendor had eluded the border guard, to seek asylum in some unknown country and from there organize a fine invasion to rescue the short wave apparatus, and if he were lucky, his wife as well.

"Don't be stupid," she said, frowning and bitter. "Nacho is in Buenos Aires working with his puppets.

And if you had had any sense, you'd be with him. Sooner or later they are going to get you."

"With your looks and my nerve, there must be a spot for the two of us on this planet. . ." Johnny said, smoothly repeating what the sausage vendor used to say when he rambled on about journeys through America.

"That means nothing now. You are being watched," she said. They were talking without looking at each other, shoulder to shoulder at the bar. Every once in a while Terelú would stick a finger in her vermouth, then suck it, reminding Johnny of a certain treachery that tortured María Félix for entire nights, the fault of Pedro Armendáriz, a fellow hard as Mexican stone, who died at the end of the movie.

"I don't care," he said, without bothering to look around. He felt very at ease with the fatalistic tone he was using, appropriate to those who are experiencing a long-awaited doom. "You think I care? No, Tere, I do not care," he repeated again. Then his voice got hoarse as he insisted nobody was going to make him change his appearance: that they wanted to do the same thing to him as the Nazis did when they tried to change a poor rustic peasant from the Rumanian quarries into a perfect specimen of the Aryan race. "And they are not going to make an Indian elephant out of me," Johnny finished.

"Where the devil did you get all that?" Terelú hissed, trying not to laugh.

"I saw it myself in a movie," Johnny said with the authority of someone who has read a book no one else has. "It was Anthony Quinn in *The 25th Hour*."

"They want to do the same to you?" she asked.

"No. But they want to turn me into a phenomenon, a bolero singer, to win summer festivals. It's almost the same," he said.

"Maybe you're right Johnny," she said.

"I *am* right. Of course I'm right," he said. "I am not going to be Mosquitos's two-headed calf," and as he finished speaking, he struck a note on the beer bottle to emphasize the drama.

"That's monstrous," said she, thinking about the calf.

"But true," said the Black. He was quiet for a moment and then recalled for Terelú the one trip he had made with Dina, to Minas one April to the Virgin of Verdún, a riotous celebration selling candles and indulgences, a mess of smoke and grease, organ music and lottery tickets, in a pleasant sacred area where you could pray to the heavens if you wanted to and enjoy yourself on earth at the same time, with gambling, part-singing contests, and drunkenness. But best of all Johnny remembered the Fiesta of Verdún for the clean breeze blowing over the faithful and for a couple of fellows who looked like Georgia preachers, calling out invitations to enter a broken-down tent and see "the last punishments of God," which actually was only one—the four-eyed gaze of an embalmed calf, with two perfect heads, found in Quebrada de los Cuervos, which presumably died when the poor animal tried to decide which way to go.

"A natural phenomenon, a punishment from God the sons-of-bitches were saying," Johnny said. "And this is the same. There are people here who can confuse you with one of those calves."

Terelú shivered, placed her warm leg next to his, and let him know that she cared for him a lot for that, that she had always believed in Johnny Sosa, that one day the whole town of Mosquitos would gather in a single well perfumed and decorated brothel, with streamers and Chinese lanterns, just to see him sing again in his best Lou Brakley style.

"The water was clear until shit fell down the pipe," Johnny said, seeing appear as if by magic at the other end of the bar, and between two characters with shaven heads, the barely distinguishable figure of the man with the bushy whiskers. "Tonight I want to sing," he said. "Bring me my ax, Tere."

The short man was stroking his heavy blue corduroy jacket with a small magpie feather in the lapel, and when he stopped talking to the two, lit a cigarette and sat down at a nearby table, to wait.

He seemed not to notice that Johnny was standing there stiff, only a few yards from him, waiting for Terelú to bring the guitar from the table by the window in the back room. By the time he raised his button eyes,

Johnny had already kicked aside the newspapers that covered the stool and was pacing back and forth, four steps each way to get used to the stage, until Terelú returned with the instrument.

"You're crazy, my Black," she said, her eyes shining. Johnny thought the polished Black Diamond was a fine guitar, Terelú a lovely woman, and the Chanteclere the best brothel in the country. Before going back to a seat at the bar, she squeezed his ebony face gently between her two hands, kissed him, found his teeth with her ample tongue, and for an instant Johnny reveled in the intensity of those poor odors of the night that used to break his heart.

When he was ready, he turned toward the audience. A block away the dogs of that dark neighborhood cocked their ears at the hearty applause arising from behind the Chanteclere's dim red light. When they heard the deep strumming of the Black Diamond, they laid their heads back down on the ground because they knew what was coming.

"You should be here to see this, Dina," Johnny was

thinking, as he resolved to begin the performance with neither "Melancholy on Your Knees" nor "*Soledad de diablo loco,*" nor sing in that language only he knew and that even so all who had seen his best days on the platform understood with no need for Spanish subtitles as in the movies.

"It is an old song from my early days, and some of you may know it in the version by Tony Rovira," Johnny explained, while he lightly adjusted the strings. Then he passed his tongue over his lips and gave an inexpressive look toward the table where the two characters were with the short man in his blue corduroy jacket. "It is called '*Mata Hari de domingo*' and goes like this," he said, and let out a scale of high and low notes, so filling the hall that it would not have occurred to anyone to substitute them, as did other singers, with the degrading introduction of percussion.

"It's good to see him," said María Teresa de Australia, chewing on her nails in the lap of a postal clerk.

"He has genius, that Black, a cheeky devil," the man who was weighing the letters said philosophically, beginning like the rest to appreciate that shaking of the knees that made words come out of Johnny's great mouth as if an angel were inside separating them into syllables before turning them loose onto the night. *"De-bes darte por ven-ci-da—si me quie-res a-tra-paar—sal-e ya de mi ca-mi-nooo,—no soy co-mo los de-máaas."* ("You might as well give up, if you want to catch me, get out of my way, I am not like the others.") When the line diminished to absolute silence to give way to the refrain, Johnny placed his open hand over the strings and filled the empty space by closing his eyes an instant. He knew when he opened them that if he turned in the direction of the women, he would be able to see reenacted the beautiful phenomenon he had observed in a few western women pioneers, who after having crossed the desert, raised their heroic gaze filled with desires to bear children as soon as they reached the first settlements of California.

Nevertheless, he did not give into this temptation. With a perfect smile, the constellation of Orion having briefly appeared between the clouds, he raised his eyelids, fixed his gaze on the bushy whiskers, and went on singing: "*Mata Hari de do-min-gooo—donde cré-es tú que vaas—pa-ra andar te fal-ta esti-looo—y destino para llegaar.*" ("Mata Hari of Sunday, where do you think you're going, to walk around you lack style, or anywhere to go.")

The short man arched an eyebrow. He didn't like having songs addressed to him, less so by a Black traitor who was making fun of the good will of Colonel Valerio and the teachings of maestro Di Giorgio aimed at making him an example for artists of decidedly low birth. One of the characters emptied his gin in a single gulp and got up smoothly, moving with his head bowed as if he didn't want to disturb anyone.

Johnny gave a nervous tremolo on the last chord and repeated with ironic tenderness: "*No me in-quieta co-nocerte — tú-no-sa-bes-quién-soy . . .yoooo,*" ("It does not worry me to know you, you don't know who I am") until he stopped, while the applause made his face seem even brighter.

With a light step among the noise of glasses and

happy commentaries, he got down off the stage and went to Terelú who was bent over her arms at the bar, sobbing.

Johnny pressed her shoulder to comfort her, wondering how best to give her some human warmth and the hope that everything would turn out all right. But she was so overly dramatic, he took out his handkerchief, covered his mouth for an instant, and then made a damp bundle, which he placed between her hands.

"Take care of this smile until I get back," he said evenly, before disappearing into the back room with the guitar in his hand and his heart beating fast.

Just as he suspected, when he crossed the curtain Johnny found himself face to face with he man who had left his table a little before the end of the song.

The fellow was alone, had one hand on his belt and the other extended in the air, as if it belonged to a wooden arm he had difficulty lowering.

"You lost, brother," the shorn head said. "The Colonel wants the guitar and the teeth."

Johnny's mouth turned dry and he felt afraid. At

his back, the conversations were returning to the gray and cloudy consistency of condemned sites; so hardly thinking, he handed over the guitar.

There was no struggle. But the shaved head had not expected Johnny to hold onto the instrument for a second in the exchange, hinting unseen meanings in that surrender, and even less would he have supposed that anyone this tightly cornered would just then flash him a smile trapped between fright and sorrow.

The shaved head was plainly disconcerted, for the dark empty face before him, with lips half-opened like the entrance of a cave, in no way resembled a universal expression of happiness.

"And the teeth?" he said, with the childlike expression of someone who has spent a night of fantasy at one of those Brazilian circuses.

Johnny shrugged his shoulders and saw the man with his two hands rigidly enclosed around the Black Diamond. He arched his back and moved past him as if there were nothing out of the ordinary, thinking only dimly of Lou Brakley when he said good-bye to his mother, pressing under his arm that famous book about the scientific search for the face of Jesus and going into the bathroom in his house in Illinois. Now Johnny walked without making a sound to the latrine by the patio, and inside, shut the whitewashed door with the latch Terelú had installed so the men would not bother the women.

That was when the short man and the other one showed up. The two were furious at each other with the dreadful helplessness of failed burglars, yelling about obedience and differences in rank. At last, their short-comings all out in the open, they came to an agreement, and shouting about how they had to find those very expensive teeth of the Black's, the three took a good while to knock down the white door to the latrine.

When they entered, with bushy whiskers swearing to God he'd blast the Black away right there, over the urinal they found only the warm odor of ammonia, minus its owner, getting weaker as it wafted through the open window of the latrine.

By now, under a black and starless sky, where only

a waning moon shone with certain humanity, Johnny was surprisingly far away. He was running like a madman, hurling himself again and again over fences, flying in agony over endless fields, breathing in the early morning, with everything his legs, which were meant for dancing, had in them.

And even though he was fleeing from Mosquitos into the countryside without having taken the precaution of checking where the devil the border that Nacho Silvera had crossed was, just the same, as out of breath and foot-sore as he was, he gave himself the pleasure of a smile to think that for the first time in his life, little as he might have expected to celebrate the event, for at least one night the two-headed calf had screwed them, and screwed them good.

Notes

Mate is the name of both the gourd and the green tea that is drunk from the gourd with a metal straw rising from a perforated bulb. Crushed leaves from the *mate* plant are packed into the gourd, hot water (with or without sugar) poured in at the mouth of the gourd, and the infusion sucked through the metal straw. *Mate* may be drunk by one person alone, or passed around among a group.

On June 26, 1973, armed forces marched through the Parliament buildings in Montevideo, evicted the members, and imposed military rule throughout the country, which lasted until the elections of 1984-5.

Johnny Sosa is planting onions a *jeme* apart, for which "span" may be the closest equivalent in English. A *jeme* is the distance between the tips of the extended thumb and forefinger.

Tejo is a game played with flat stones, either thrown against a line, or into a container.

Francisco Acuña de Figueroa is the author of the verses that in 1833 were officially declared the national anthem, beginning *"Orientales, la patria o la tumba!"* He also published clandestinely a long pornographic poem titled *"Apología del carajo,"* or "Apology for the Prick," that listed a hundred-some words for the *carajo.* The poem circulated again in the last year of the dictatorship.